ANIMALIA
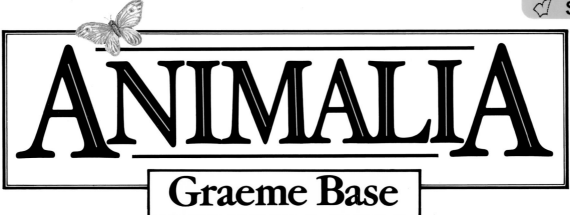

Graeme Base

Within the pages of this book
You may discover, if you look
Beyond the spell of written words,
A hidden land of beasts and birds.

For many things are 'of a kind',
And those with keenest eyes will find
A thousand things, or maybe more —
It's up to you to keep the score.

A final word before we go;
There's one more thing you ought to know:
In Animalia, you see,
It's possible you might find *me*.

— Graeme

For Robyn

Puffin Books

An Armoured Armadillo Avoiding An Angry Alligator

DIABOLICAL DRAGONS
DAINTILY DEVOURING
DELICIOUS DELICACIES

FOUR
FAT
FROGS
FISHING
—FOR—
FRIGHTENED
FISH

GREAT GREEN GORILLAS GROWING GRAPES IN A GORGEOUS GLASS GREENHOUSE

Horrible **hairy hogs** hurrying homeward on heavily-harnessed horses

INGENIOUS
IGUANAS
IMPROVISING AN INTRICATE IMPROMPTU ON IMPOSSIBLY IMPRACTICAL INSTRUMENTS

JOVIAL · JACKALS · JUGGLING · JUGS · OF · JELLY · IN · THE · JUNGLE ·

Nine Nautical Newts
Navigating
Near Norway

ONE
OUTRAGEOUS
OLD
OSTRICH
ORDERING
AN
ONION
OMELETTE

Proud Peacocks

Preening Perfect Plumage

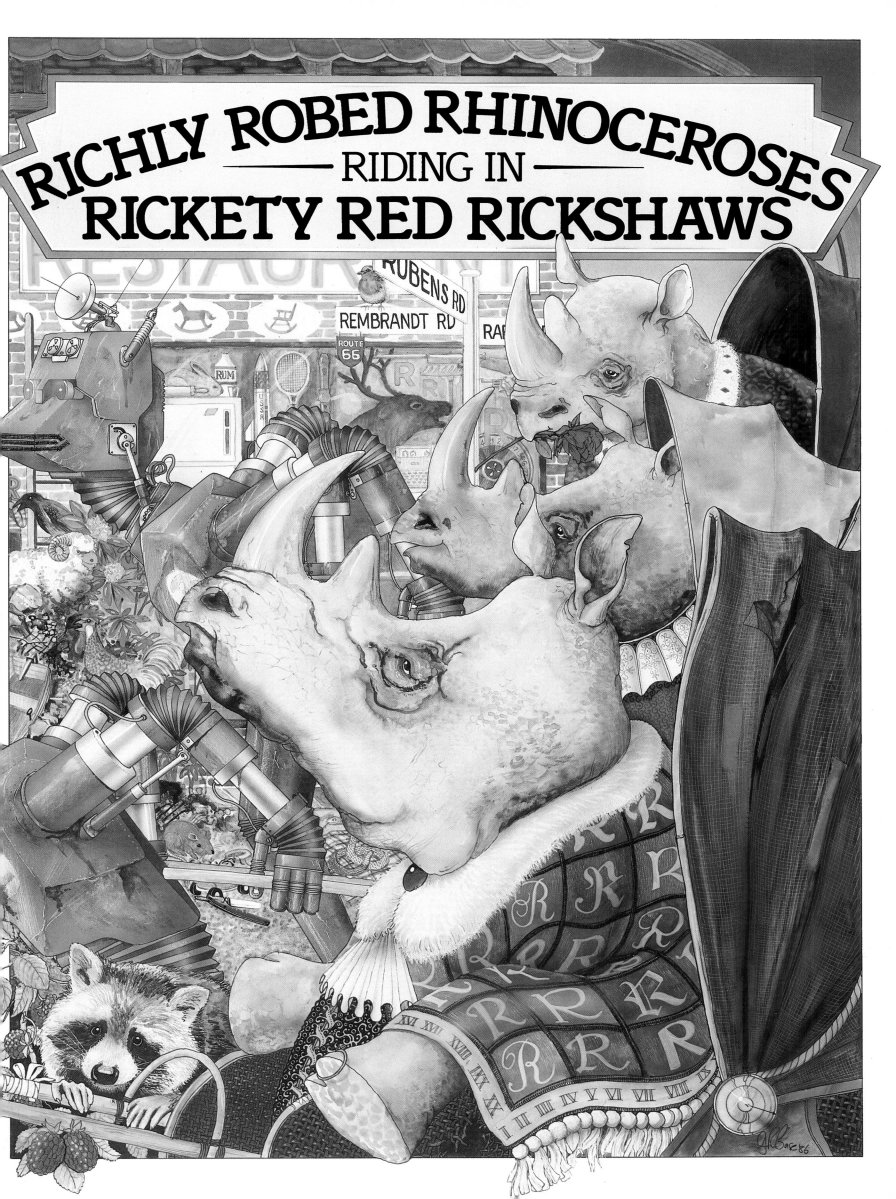

SIX · SLITHERING · SNAKES
SLIDING · SILENTLY · SOUTHWARD

TWO TIGERS TAKING THE 10.20 TRAIN TO TIMBUKTU

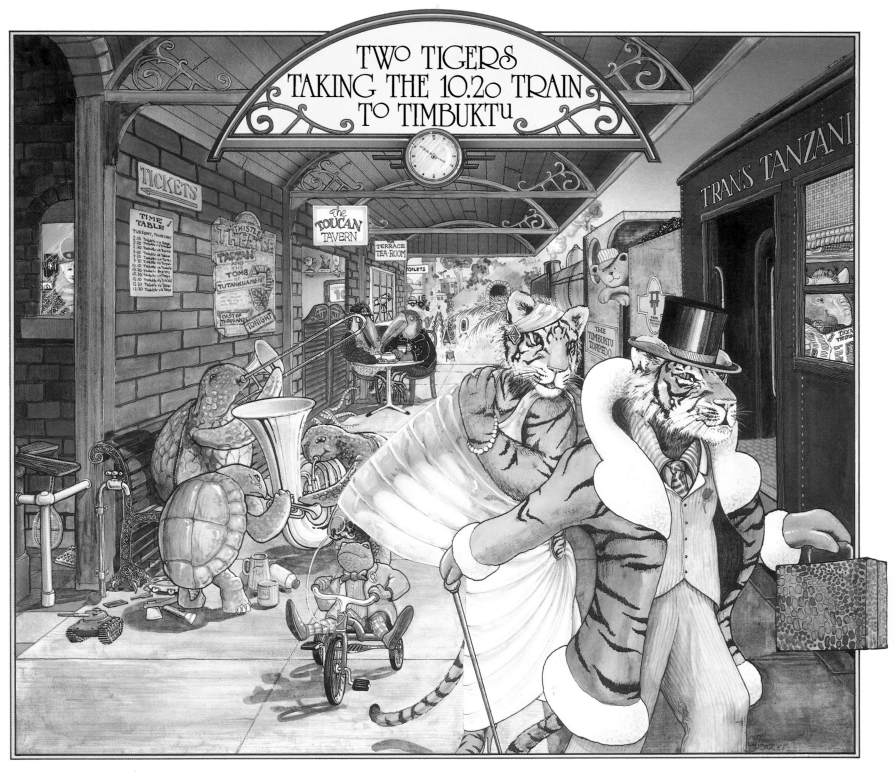

UNRULY UNICORNS UPENDING URNS OF ULTRAMARINE UMBRELLAS

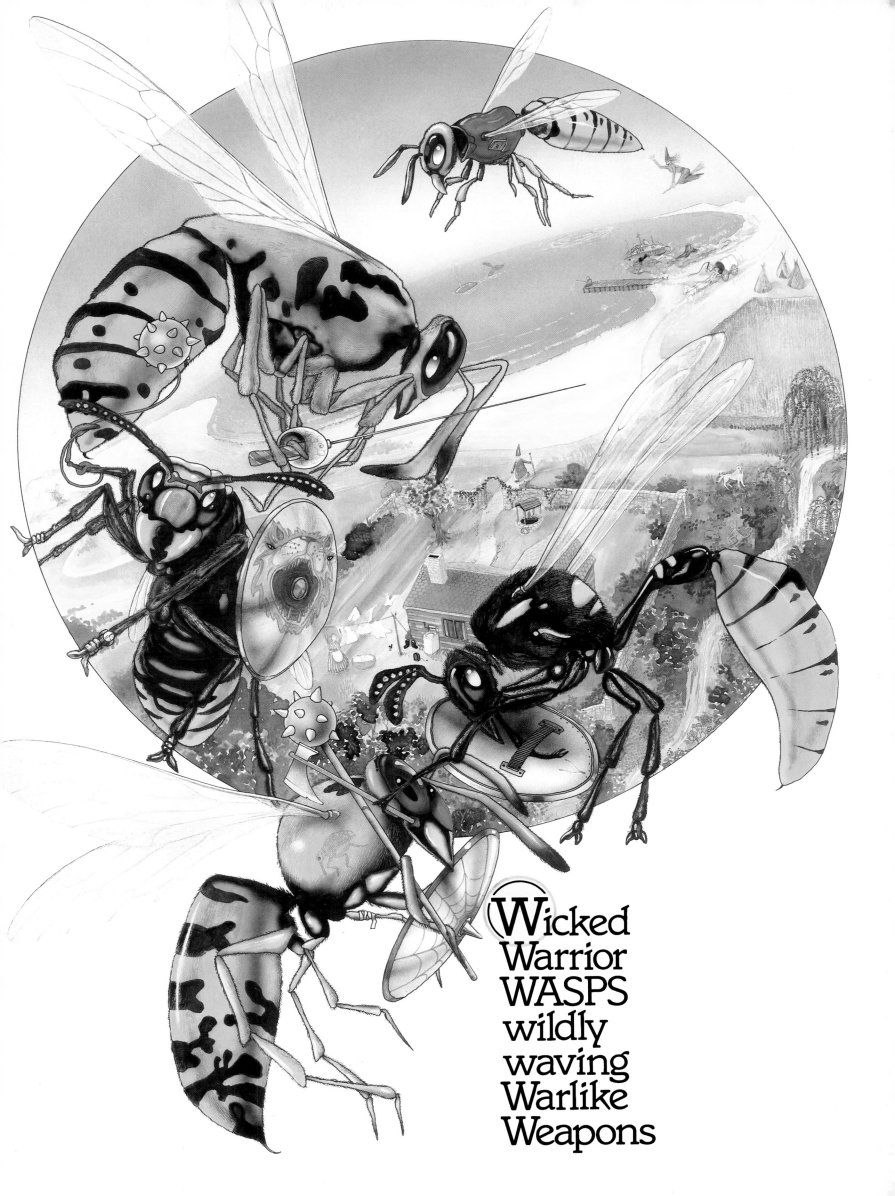

Wicked
Warrior
WASPS
wildly
waving
Warlike
Weapons

**YOUTHFUL YAKS YODELLING
IN YELLOW YACHTS**

Z.
ZANY ZEBRAS ZIGZAGGING IN ZINC ZEPPELINS

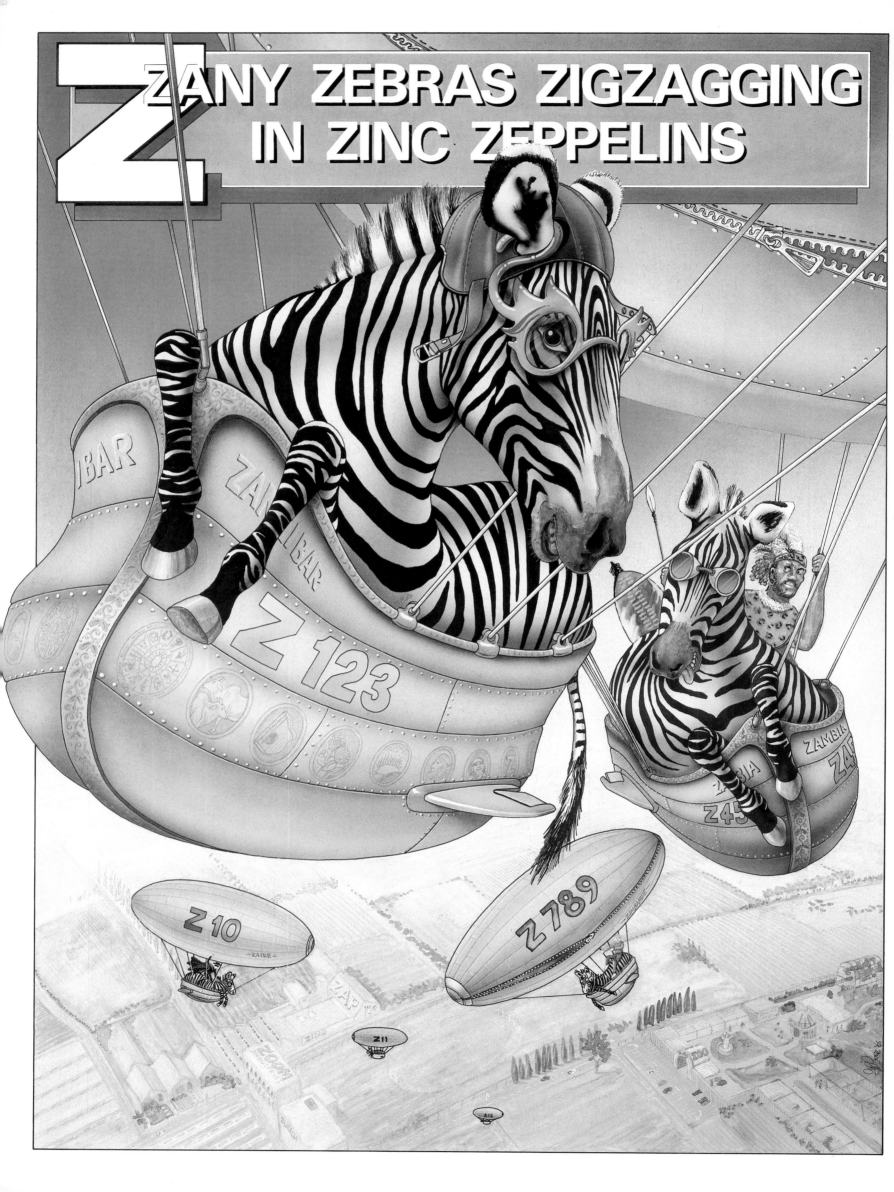